Invasion!

Jonas Hassen Khemiri

Translated by
Rachel Willson-Broyles

A SAMUEL FRENCH ACTING EDITION

FOUNDED 1830

SAMUELFRENCH.COM
SAMUELFRENCH-LONDON.CO.UK

ISBN 978-0-573-70067-5

www.SamuelFrench.com
www.SamuelFrench-London.co.uk

MUSIC USE NOTE

Licensees are solely responsible for obtaining formal written permission from copyright owners to use copyrighted music in the performance of this play and are strongly cautioned to do so. If no such permission is obtained by the licensee, then the licensee must use only original music that the licensee owns and controls. Licensees are solely responsible and liable for all music clearances and shall indemnify the copyright owners of the play(s) and their licensing agent, Samuel French, against any costs, expenses, losses and liabilities arising from the use of music by licensees. Please contact the appropriate music licensing authority in your territory for the rights to any incidental music.

IMPORTANT BILLING AND CREDIT REQUIREMENTS

If you have obtained performance rights to this title, please refer to your licensing agreement for important billing and credit requirements.

INVASION! was first produced in the original Swedish at the Stockholms Stadsteater in Stockholm, Sweden, running from March 2006 to January 2008, with set and costume design by Zofi Nilsson, lighting design by William Wenner, sound design by Mattias Gustafsson and Maria Skoog, and makeup design by Patricia Svajger. It was directed by Farnaz Arbabi, with the following cast:

Shebly Niavarani

Bashkim Neziraj

Isabel Munshi

Bahador Foladi

INVASION! , as translated by Rachel Willson-Broyles, was presented in its American premiere by The Play Company, Founding Producer Kate Loewald and Executive Producer Lauren Weigel, at Walkerspace in New York City on February 21, 2011, with set design by Antje Ellermann, costume design by Oana Botez-Ban, lighting design by Matthew Richards, sound design by Bart Fasbender, fight choreography by J. Steven White, and production stage management by April Ann Kline. It was directed and adapted for the New York stage by Erica Schmidt with the following cast:

Andrew Ramcharan Guilarte

Francis Benhamou

Bobby Moreno

Debargo Sanyal

This translation was revived by The Play Company at The Flea Theater in New York City on September 13, 2011, with set design by Antje Ellermann, costume design by Oana Botez-Ban, lighting design by Matthew Richards, sound design by Bart Fasbender, fight choreography by J. Steven White, and production stage management by Larry K. Ash. It was directed and adapted for the New York stage by Erica Schmidt with the following cast:

Andrew Ramcharan Guilarte

Francis Benhamou

Bobby Moreno

Nick Choksi

CHARACTERS

A – man, 40-50 years old – **ACTOR 1, LANCE, GUIDE, JOURNALIST, APPLE PICKER**

B – man, 20-25 years old – **ARVIND, EXPERT 1, FANON-LOVER**

C – woman, 20-25 years old – **ACTOR 2, LARA, EXPERT 2, INTERPRETER**

D – man, 20-25 years old – **YOUSEF, ALEXANDRA, ERIC, EXPERT 3, ANTI-NUCLEAR LADY, LITTLE BROTHER**

LENGTH OF PLAY

Preferably not longer than two hours.

AUTHOR'S NOTES

Riddle: Who is really hiding in the experts' names?

In the Foyer

(YOUSEF and ARVIND come into the foyer from the street, wearing caps and sweatpants. They each have a McDonald's straw and some paper napkins; they're blowing wads of paper at each other. Pushing each other into other patrons, giving threatening looks if anyone says anything to them. Walking around the foyer, being loud, hitting on some girl ["hey girl, you're fine, come sit with us, we have VIP seats, yo"].)

Scene One
Almquist's Intro

(The audience in. **YOUSEF** *and* **ARVIND** *are sitting next to each other, near the stage.* **ACTOR 1** *and* **ACTOR 2** *are performing a scene from Carl Jonas Love Almquist's* Signora Luna. *Theatric tone, big gestures.* **YOUSEF** *and* **ARVIND** *snicker, disturbing the serious atmosphere.)*

A/ACTOR 1. Don Silvio Luna sailed with his consort away
And his daughter with them from Italy's dry land
One blissful summer, away to Sardinia,
Where as in a fair chivalrous tale, on high cliffs
In Mediterranean view his castle stood.
Not long the road to Cagliari town, and here
From the wreath, full of plaited holly and olive
Into the sky rose the spires of Luna's castle

(Sounds of wind and ill-boding strings. **YOUSEF** *and* **ARVIND** *start to whisper to each other.)*

C/ACTOR 2. That summer, driven by wind, a Corsair Arab
Made his journey from Africa up to the north
He came for spoils, and anchored at Sardinia's sand
He went ashore, and donna Antonia caught his eye

*(***YOUSEF** *and* **ARVIND** *start to ask other audience members if they understand what's being said onstage.)*

A/ACTOR 1. He did not seize his lady with violence; he lay
With heart so warm three days at the breast of the coast
Never had his flag not waved in delight so long!
Still one day more he lingered there with ship and men.

C/ACTOR 2. He captivated his lady's bright happy heart
Without consent on her mother's or father's part
Italy's soil must remember the Arab's name.
He was from Northwest Africa, of Maghreb tribe
He, Abulkasem…

A/ACTOR 1. The famous pillager?

 The torcher of Italy's islands, him?

C/ACTOR. *(nods)* ABULKASEM ALI MOHARREM

 (**ARVIND** *makes a farting noise,* **YOUSEF** *laughs.*)

A/ACTOR 1. Away he sailed on the evening of the fourth day,

 And away Antonia Luna followed free.

 From the Arab's wealth she adorned hair and arm

 With pearls, robbed away off of Christian women's heads

 Two years on – for so hastily, the tale has led

 Though darkly – two years on…

 Abulkasem with his craft went into Corfu

 A Greek island to the east of Amalfi town.

 It was in the time we fought the Arabs' power

 Of the empire in Sicily; that time I knew

 A boy myself – we won battles back and forth then.

 But Abulkasem, he was one of those, one time,

 Who was forced to himself retreat away, his wounds…

 (**ARVIND** *makes a loud farting noise,* **ACTORS 1 & 2** *lose their place.*)

C/ACTOR 2. If everyone could just show a little respect, we are…

B/ARVIND. Hey, *you* should show respect, yo.

A/ACTOR 1. If you can't behave properly, then there's no point in us…

D/YOUSEF. *(as though he's yelling an insult)* Properly? You're proper, you're proper!!!

 (**YOUSEF** *and* **ARVIND** *rush up on the stage, knocking down* **ACTOR 1,** *who is helped off the stage by* **ACTOR 2.** *The play is interrupted, the lights come on, the stage manager yells "Call security!" as* **YOUSEF** *and* **ARVIND** *take over the stage and tear down the scenery.* **YOUSEF** *finds a megaphone)*

D/YOUSEF. *(through the megaphone)* We would like to inform you that Mr. Christensen, our teacher, is a huge whore and he sucks dick and has elephant balls…One two one two are there any real brothers in the house or is it just a bunch of theater fags?

B/ARVIND. Who owns the show now, bitches? Who's Shakespeare?

D/YOUSEF. Who's Shakespeare now, bitches? Who IS?

B/ARVIND. A-a-and to that bitch out in the hall who said something like…

D/YOUSEF. *(imitating the lady)* She called you "Slumdog Millionaire"…? don't think we didn't hear!

B/ARVIND. Right, just so you know Slumdog is running the show now…

(short pause)

(to the audience, suddenly without an accent) This is how it all begins. We're at the theater with our class. It's the first play I've seen in my life. And it's total shit…

*(**ACTOR 1** back out on the stage.)*

A/ACTOR 1. *(exaggeratedly formal theatric voice)* Don Silvio Luna sailed with his blah blah
And his daughter blah, blah from Italy's blah blah…

B/ARVIND. I start to do my sick fart trick and everyone cracks up, especially Yousef. The play is interrupted, the actors leave the stage, and we make our attack while Mr. Christensen, our teacher, yells…

D/MR. CHRISTENSEN. NOOOOO!

B/ARVIND. Soon the cops show up and we're hauled out to the street and one of the cops slugs Eric…

*(resounding clap from **YOUSEF**)*

But we fight back and Eric kicks one of the cops in the kneecap and Alexandra rips off his name tag and the last thing we hear as we run like crazy for the subway is Mr. Christensen's voice, shouting like…

D/MR. CHRISTENSEN. *(beseeching)* See you tomorrow!

   (short pause)

B/ARVIND. It was the last time we saw Mr. Christensen. The next day we're sitting in the classroom waiting and he doesn't show up. He has quit...he broke down...just like all the others. Truthfully, we're a little ashamed, but no one wants to admit it so we slide on down to the lunchroom and play cards instead. Yousef is the first guy to talk about the play...

D/YOUSEF. Hey listen, that play yesterday, *Señorita Luna* by that Almquist guy. Wasn't it maaaaad wack!

B/ARVIND. And everyone just. Yeah totally.

D/YOUSEF. Wasn't it mighty mighty shit!

B/ARVIND. Sure.

D/YOUSEF. Bro, it sucked elephant balls, am I right?

B/ARVIND. Yeah, it was bad, we know...

D/YOUSEF. I mean it was so sucky that...

B/ARVIND. Hey! We know, aight? That's enough...And then something shady happens that I'll never forget. I have this super strong memory of how Yousef is sitting there, this little Christian Lebanese guy with this awesome lumberjack 'stache, with the cards like this in a huge fan. And with like this little kind of shamed face he says...

D/YOUSEF. But isn't Abulkasem a sweet name?

B/ARVIND. And he really says it like...

D/YOUSEF. *(slow motion)* Sweeeeeeet name.

B/ARVIND. And everyone in the lunchroom just gets quiet and then...

D/ALEXANDRA & B/ARVIND. *(laughing)*
WOOOOOOOOOOOOOOOOOOOO!

B/ARVIND. We just laugh and call him a theater nerd and Alexandra says Yousef's mom gets a visit from Abulkasem every night and Yousef is all...

D/YOUSEF. No, no, I just mean like, I just mean his name, like, I have an uncle in Lebanon called Abulkasem!

*(When **YOUSEF** says the name Abulkasem we leave the lunchroom and the stage fills with smoke. We get to see **YOUSEF**'s memories of his dancing uncle Abulkasem, better known as **LANCE**.)*

A/LANCE. *(singing in a tune similar to "I'm Too Sexy" by Right Said Fred.)**

I'm too sexy for your land too sexy for your land
New York and also France

D/YOUSEF. *(to the audience)* My uncle!

*(**LANCE** dances and struts.)*

My uncle Abulkasem!

A/LANCE. *(interrupting)* Lance! My name is Lance…

D/YOUSEF. Sorry. Lance.

*(**LANCE** continues to strut.)*

"Lance" was his "stage name" that he used here in New York. His greatest dream was to become a dancer… The problem was, of course, that only we knew about Lance's dreams. In real life, his name was still Abulkasem and he lived in Lebanon, where suspicious neighbors whispered about his disinterest in marriage. He worked as some sort of termite exterminator… drifting around all day in the suburbs of Beirut with his canister backpack and his gasmask, spraying pests to death…all to save up enough cash to come visit us at Christmas.

*(**LANCE** sings more from "I'm Too Sexy" by Right Said Fred.)***

Abulkasem!

A/LANCE. Lance!

D/YOUSEF. Lance…Lance-Albukasem…who had like…a hybrid stink. Sweat and Obsession in some kind of

---

*Please see Music Use Note on Page 3.
**Please see Music Use Note on Page 3.

crazy strong combination...He came every Christmas when I was little...some well-groomed damn huggy dude with hairy muscle legs who always insisted on walking around in only a tank top and underwear at home in our kitchen. Abulkasem...The dog lover...I remember one time, on the street, he said hi to one of those gigantic bear-like monster dogs, he just petted it all over and let it lick his face and I was so impressed. Abulkasem...who tried on fancy shiny shoes in stores that we didn't dare go into and sometimes spent whole nights somewhere other than the sofa that mom made up for him, and he always, here in New York, always introduced himself as Lance, a struggling dancer.

When his vacation was over, Lance went home to Beirut and became Abulkasem again, who chased termites and wrote thank-you letters...

I remember the last time Lance came for a visit...As usual, we picked him up at JFK and as usual he came gliding out of customs with a huge smile on his face, with perfume billowing around him, and everyone hugged and no one said anything about Lance's belly, which had gotten bigger, or about the steadily growing bare spot on his head.

A/LANCE. Wow Yousef, you've grown so much and Dalilla, my queen of a sister, always more beautiful than a summer rain! And Samir, my king of a brother-in-law. There you are.

D/YOUSEF. When the Christmas celebration was done with, Lance got ready to travel upstate to:

A/LANCE. Take in the country air darlings...

D/YOUSEF. He was as gushingly happy as usual and danced down to the train station one Friday afternoon.

A/LANCE. See you later, alligators!

D/YOUSEF. The apartment was creepily quiet without him. I even think dad missed his perfumed presence.

Lance was going to come back on Sunday and we went all together to meet him at Grand Central. We saw

him from a distance and...This is probably my abso-
lute strongest memory of Lance...That sparkling smile
in the middle of all the winter-tired New Yorkers, his
cone-shaped body and that fluttering apricot-colored
waistcoat he'd gotten on sale...He like soared toward
us...As though he had a rocket-powered backpack...
And it wasn't until he had gotten close and we were
going to hug that I saw something was different...But
no one said anything...No one said anything...

(YOUSEF *smiles.*)

We just stood there like idiots and listened as Lance
gushed about how wonderful his trip had been...

A/LANCE. Snow like a blanket...my Saturday constitutional
in the forest...such joy!

D/YOUSEF. ...The train ride back...The nice soldiers in the
same car –

A/LANCE. – they offered me alcohol from a can...and had
a music player!...they laughed, I sang...I sang, they
laughed. Sleep overtook me in the early morning
hours...

D/YOUSEF. The rest of the train trip that had been just as
nice, with smiles and more smiles from everyone.

(**YOUSEF** *continues to smile as though it's a funny story.*)

And none of us said anything. We just stood there
and listened to his babbling...Because honestly, what
could we say? How could we say it? Who would lead
Abulkasem up to a mirror and show him that someone, on the train, had taken a marker and drawn long
black whiskers that went like this, all the way from his
upper lip to his earlobes. Who would show him that
someone had turned the tip of his nose into a black
dot? And also written two words on his forehead, right
over his well-plucked eyebrows? Go Home.

He discovered it himself when we got into the car...

(**YOUSEF** *smiles, shaking his head.*)

A/LANCE. Go home? What means? Go home? Why...

D/YOUSEF. Mom lied to him, of course...said that it was some kind of American welcome tradition...like that you offer someone alcohol and draw whiskers and write go home on each other's foreheads.

C/MOM. Yes, go home, haven't you all heard? This means you *are* home, this is your home, *now*, you stay, you are welcome ...

(**YOUSEF** *loses his thread, smiles in a forced manner.*)

D/YOUSEF. It was the best thing mom could think of...you are welcome...Dad just drove and said...nothing.

(*The stream of memories ends.* **LANCE** *exits the stage. We're back in the lunchroom.*)

(*to* **ARVIND**) No no, I just mean like, I mean his name, I mean I have an uncle in Lebanon named Abulkasem... who's a huge Mafioso...I mean that's why...

B/ARVIND. And we just get kind of quiet and then...

D/ALEXANDRA & B/ARVIND. (*laughing*)
WOOOOOOOOOOOOO!

(*short pause*)

B/ARVIND. From that day on, Abulkasem becomes like an expression in our class...

D/YOUSEF. But you have to admit that Abulkasem is a sweet name...

B/ARVIND. Soon became...

D/YOUSEF. But admit Abulkasem is sweet.

B/ARVIND. Which soon became...

D/YOUSEF. Admit Abulkasem.

B/ARVIND. It turned into one of those things that we started to say, first mostly as a joke but then more serious... On breaks we shot some hoops or sat in the hall and smoked Smarties and then someone would just say...

D/YOUSEF. Admit Abulkasem!

B/ARVIND. And everyone would just crack up because... I don't know why...It was just so goddamn fucking funny. Soon Abulkasem was its own word. At first it

meant something that was wack, weak, lame, warped...
Hey bro, how was that party last weekend?

D/YOUSEF. *(complaining)* I swear man, it was Abulkasem. No
hos, just a bunch of white boys, we split early.

B/ARVIND. Then, after a few weeks, the meaning of the
word changed and started to mean something that was
awesome, phat, crazy good...

D/YOUSEF. *(happily)* I swear, he was totally Abulkasem! He
got fourteen in the first quarter.

B/ARVIND. And later in the semester, like some time in
December, when we'd gotten a new substitute, and
Alexandra got kicked out of school after...

*(YOUSEF signals with his hand across his throat and
discreet head-shaking that ARVIND should censure the
story.)*

Uh...some crap with the shop teacher. Then Abulkasem
could mean absolutely anything. It could be an adjec-
tive...

D/YOUSEF. *(yawning)* Shit, I'm mad Abulkasem. I was up
watching movies all night...

B/ARVIND. Verb...

D/YOUSEF. *(irritated)* Come on, Mr. Anderson, Abulkasem
someone else, I didn't have time to study...

B/ARVIND. It could be an insult...

D/YOUSEF. *(threatening)* Don't play Abulkasem, man, no
cuts, it was my turn.

B/ARVIND. It could be a compliment...

D/YOUSEF. Hey, check out the chica, Look! She's nice yo,
she's slim fit, she's flo-jo, she's crazy Abulkasem, admit
it!

B/ARVIND. It became the perfect word. But of course sometimes there were misunderstandings...

D/YOUSEF. *(angrily)* What the fuck you mean, Abulkasem?
Oh, okay, you mean *Abulkasem. (apologetically)* Okay, my
bad.

B/**ARVIND**. But most of the time you understood the context. Lots of things were like that then...words changed and evolved. But the funny thing was, lots of other words like knatch or skrilla or shooli or chedda were ones that were overused and then disappeared. Everyone said it for a month and then one day it was just...

D/**YOUSEF**. What did you say? Are you still calling skrilla chedda? Nigga please, that's so ancient.

B/**ARVIND**. The strange thing about Abulkasem was that the word stuck around, it changed, it grew, it lived on...

(short pause)

High school becomes college, the old gang from school is split up, Yousef moves out of the city to study to be a dentist, Alexandra is lost to drugs. I start working as a telemarketer and only still keep in touch with Eric...we see each other now and then...Go into the city, have a couple beers, talk memories, update each other on what's going on with old homies. On one such night we meet at this bar, one of those regular chill places, not super classy but still chill, you know...cozy...We're standing there chatting when I suddenly see Her...

D/**ERIC**. Hello? What's wrong?

B/**ARVIND**. Look...look over there...

*(**LARA** enters the stage.)*

D/**ERIC**. What?

B/**ARVIND**. Don't you see? Check out that chick...Check out the friendina! DAMN!

D/**ERIC**. That girl? That rich chick in grunge? For fuck's sake, pull yourself together...

B/**ARVIND**. Can't you see her? Shit, she's fine. *(to the audience)* She's just come in from the street and she's alone and...I don't know...How can you describe someone like her? Maybe if you were black you would just slide right up and just...

D/BLACK. Yo baby yo baby yo baby YO! You must be tired cause you've been running around my brain all day.

B/ARVIND. And maybe if you were Mexican you'd just sneak up and whisper…

D/MEXICAN. I tink you are veeery pretty, I want you come home with me.

B/ARVIND. And maybe if you were white boy you'd chug twelve or fourteen beers and just…

D/WHITE BOY. *(unintelligible slurring)*

B/ARVIND. That's how fine she is. Dark curls and super sexy lips and a little cute kind of snub nose and a style that just radiates class…This is no damn hood rat, this is top shelf, classy style, you know one of those girls who studies university and has parents with BMWs and lives condo and buys unlimited subway pass and has a gym membership that she barely uses and hangs on her summers in Hamptons and DAMN! She is fine! Kapow! Hubba hubba! Grr! *(siren sounds, panting sounds)*

D/ERIC. Go talk to her, then…

B/ARVIND. No…Eh, that's not my style, you know.

D/ERIC. Come on, Arvind…Come on, man, don't play Abulkasem. Slide on up to her.

B/ARVIND. She moves toward the bar and like magic my beer is empty… *(desperately chugs his beer)* I get up on nervous knees, wipe my sweaty hands on my jeans. There she is. I move closer, toast my empty bottle in the air, and smile my magical smile… *(wobbly, stammering teen voice)* Oh…and what might we be called?

C/LARA. What?

B/ARVIND. Wh-wh-what's your name?

C/LARA. *(bored)* Lara…And yours?

B/ARVIND. And I'm just "Oh, oh, get some water – someone here is hot like fire" you know…And I…I'm just about to say my name when I catch sight of Eric over at the table, raising his thumb like the worst hitchhiker…

*(**ERIC** gives a thumbs up and exits the stage.)*

And…I don't know why but I just can't say Arvind… I've always hated it…Shit, I've gotten teased so much because of it. Everyone's all: "What did you say? Is your name Arvid?" Fuck no. ARVIND. With an N!!! I just can't handle the same explanation I've repeated my whole life. "Not Arvid: ARVIND, it's an Indian name, my family is from…yadda yadda yadda"…so instead I lean toward her and say: "My name is…Abulkasem."

C/LARA. Abulkasem?

B/ARVIND. Abulkasem…

C/LARA. Abulkasem…Really? That's your name?

B/ARVIND. Yes.

C/LARA. Did you know there's an Abulkasem in *Arabian Nights*?

B/ARVIND. *(suddenly completely calm)* "Sure. Of course. But it's most famous from that play. You know, *Seniorluna*… by that Almquist guy." And it's like a giant lightning strike…the transformation is complete…Suddenly it's not the nervous, girl-shy Arvind who's standing there…It's not Arvind who was teased for his stutter or his nerd name. It's Abulkasem! I am Abulkasem! The name like takes over and fills me with calmness. Abulkasem is crazy confident…Abulkasem has no shaky sweating, no wobbly knees…Abulkasem just keeps the girl next to the bar and starts to soothe her ears with the most excellent compliments. "You…You are fine…Damn fine, I mean…Really…"

C/LARA. *(suddenly loving)* Thanks…God, what a nice thing to say…

B/ARVIND. Abulkasem tells about his flashy telemarketing job…Abulkasem asks interesting questions like a super pro pimp…He offers cigs and cracks great jokes and offers to pay for her beer. Everything is nice mood and best atmosphere. Up until she gets a bad conscience about her friends…

C/LARA. Hey, I have to go find my friends…But…Maybe we can talk a little more later?

B/ARVIND. And Abulkasem gets just what she means…You know…"Talk a little more later"…In girl talk…I swear she's hot, she wants me. So I'm like: "Sure…You can just give me your number so we can…'talk later'"…

C/LARA. Okay…I'll write it here…Take care…But promise you'll call…

(**LARA** *exits the stage, with a flirty smile.*)

B/ARVIND. I swear that's the last thing she says before she goes over to her friends. And I just…or Abulkasem just…Or both of us stand there with the cell number in hand and then we slide back over to Eric with two newly bought beers and toast with our bottles and everything is just so damn beautiful you know one of those nights when everything just sparkles and shines and lives and crackles and you even smile at bouncers…One of those nights when bus drivers let you ride home for free and the winter is starting to smell like spring and your thoughts on the way home whisper… Finally…Finally things are starting to change…It was a night like that…An awesome night…

Scene Two
The Panel of Experts on Abulkasem's Birth

A/GUIDE. I would like to extend a warm welcome to our viewers at home and I am very, very glad to see so many here. You can think of me as a little bit like... your guide for the evening. My steady hand will lead you through the evening and if anything is unclear, absolutely anything, just grab me and ask. Okay? Okay...And remember...There are *no* stupid questions...Abulkasem...That man of many myths...Who was he, really? What did his life look like before he became one of the world's most sought-after men? Let us begin at the beginning and just keep to the facts... Let us drill our way through the fiction in order to reveal the truth about Abulkasem...To help us, we have our panel of eminent experts. Applause!

(**EXPERTS** 1, 2, and 3 *enter the stage.*)

A warm welcome...My first question...Where was Abulkasem born?

B/EXPERT 1. We believe he was born in Tair Harfa, a village situated in what is now southern Lebanon. Robin Alty has depicted Abulkasem's childhood in the television documentary *Down From Day One.*

C/EXPERT 2. But we also know that Hugo Sbeger, in his extraordinary biography *The Radiance of Abulkasem,* presents findings that indicate that Abulkasem was actually born on Palestinian ground, in the village of al-Birwa.

D/EXPERT 3. Yes...That is to say...If he wasn't born in al-Bassa or Iqrit, as professor Chi Yen Deck argues.

A/GUIDE. So what do we know about his childhood? Was he shy? Aggressive? Did he have many friends?

C/EXPERT 2. As Hugo Sbeger accurately states, Abulkasem's childhood was, and I quote, "as average as a childhood can be without becoming exceptional in its mediocrity", end quote.

D/EXPERT 3. Dr. Cecil Zeenoza says that Abulkasem was the youngest of eight siblings. He was born, grew up, lived a completely average life in a completely average refugee camp.

A/GUIDE. How was he at school then? Do we know?

B/EXPERT 1. In a paper that was presented at Wits University in Johannesburg, Alfred Dunmolds, one of the world's most reputable experts, writes that Abulkasem often sat in the middle of the classroom. Not in the back row; not in front.

C/EXPERT 2. He was one of those students that his classmates had trouble remembering only a few years after graduation.

D/EXPERT 3. A little bit anonymous.

C/EXPERT 2. A little bit like a shadow.

B/EXPERT 1. Without any real characteristics.

C/EXPERT 2. Someone who was soon reduced to a vague sense of recognition, you know, one of those classmates you see in an elevator ten years later without saying hi.

D/EXPERT 3. And only after you've left the elevator do you realize why that person's face was so familiar.

B/EXPERT 1. But at that point the elevator doors have just closed and it's too late.

A/THE GUIDE. Hmm…So there's nothing in Abulkasem's childhood that can explain his violent future? No weapons? No fundamentalism?

C/EXPERT 2. Not yet. As a youth, Abulkasem is still naively untouched.

B/EXPERT 1. Although…Chi Yen Deck points out that Abulkasem's father was very hateful. He beat his wife and assaulted his daughters.

D/EXPERT 3. Precisely. "It was a perfect breeding ground for terrorism", writes Deck in the biography published by Doubleday in 1987.

A/THE GUIDE. Yes, terrorism. What do we actually know about Abulkasem's political engagement?

B/EXPERT 1. Robin Alty says that Abulkasem is twenty-four years old when he's hired as a columnist for the Arabic newspaper El-Kharion. And this is when his troubles begin. Under thinly-veiled pseudonyms like Akulbasem or Alubkasem he starts to write his much-discussed columns...

D/EXPERT 3. He embraces American foreign policy.

C/EXPERT 2. He defends Israel's expanded settlements; he thanks the Israelis, those landless people, for taking pity on Palestine, that people-less land.

B/EXPERT 1. But at the same time we know that Abulkasem marches in anti-American demonstrations, chants anti-Semitic slurs, and burns the Israeli flag. All according to Hugo Sbeger.

A/GUIDE. So in other words his columns are ironic...right?

D/EXPERT 3. We believe so.

B/EXPERT 1. What we KNOW, however, is that from this point on, NO ONE can depend upon Abulkasem.

C/EXPERT 2. He becomes the master of flip-flopping.

D/EXPERT 3. He soon becomes known as a collaborator among his countrymen.

C/EXPERT 2. And as a member of the resistance in enemy camps.

B/EXPERT 1. The western world sees him as a potential terrorist...

C/EXPERT 2. The Arab world as a traitor.

D/EXPERT 3. Everyone reads him as an opponent.

B/EXPERT 1. And soon everyone agrees that Abulkasem is the greatest threat to our common future.

A/GUIDE. And this is where the hunt begins?

C/EXPERT 2. Exactly.

A/GUIDE. Thank you very much...Now we'll take a break... We'll be back after this...

Scene Three
The Demon Director

(**LARA** *is alone on the stage, wearing riding boots and a riding helmet.*)

C/**LARA.** The monologue starts with me standing outside my door and swearing so much it echoes in the stairwell. Fucking goddamn cuntcock! For the third time in two weeks I've managed to lock myself out. What a craptastic idiotic dumbfuck. Why is life so...typical? All week I've been so fucking productive; I studied for exams, helped my brother move, managed not to go out, helped out instead, took an exam...I've even defrosted the freezer! Mostly to avoid studying, but still! Can you imagine a more productive person? And still I'm standing here now, leaning forward and sweating, in squeaking riding boots, looking in through my own mail slot. Again. Unholy shitsucking fucktard.

I collect myself. Take a deep breath. I decide to go by the bar where my seminar group is celebrating being done with the exam. I'd actually planned to stay home, but now I would so much rather have a beer than call the locksmith. Again. He would crack his joke about how I should get a punch card from him. Again. And I would pretend to laugh in the hope of getting one. Again.

The bar we're going to is called Kelly's, maybe you know it? A fucking shitty cheap beer dive. We're talking neon signs in the window, angry bouncers, we're talking beer bottles in buckets, like two bucks apiece. Bon Jovi music, sports fans, and cougars in leather skirts. I slip in. Look for my seminar group...move toward the bar to order...Then suddenly I feel how someone starts to pull the shark move...You know...Someone starts to like circle around and around with a hungry gaze...

(**ARVIND** *circles around* **LARA** *with a sexy expression.*)

Of course. Just what I need. A flirt-happy Turk in a leather vest...

(ARVIND tests his breath against his palm and slides up.)

B/ARVIND. *(stammering)* W-w-what's up baby?

C/LARA. What?

B/ARVIND. What up? I'm Abulkasem…How's it hangin'? What up?

C/LARA. What?

B/ARVIND. I mean…I'm Abulkasem…How's it going?

C/LARA. Oh, it's okay.

B/ARVIND. Mellow.

C/LARA. *(to the bartender)* Excuse me, can I order? A Pilsner, please.

(embarrassing silence)

B/ARVIND. So…are things good, or…?

C/LARA. Yes, thanks. They're fine.

B/ARVIND. I like your boots.

C/LARA. Uh…thanks.

B/ARVIND. *(nodding toward LARA's riding helmet)* Do you ride a moped or something?

C/LARA. No.

B/ARVIND. Good.

C/LARA. Why is that good?

B/ARVIND. What?

C/LARA. Why is it good that I don't ride a moped?

B/ARVIND. I mean…I don't either.

C/LARA. So?

B/ARVIND. Well, so we have something in common. Besides, I have my driver's license, you know, and I can borrow a company car if I want.

C/LARA. Okay.

(Embarrassing silence. LARA receives her beer.)

B/ARVIND. I work in telemarketing myself. Sweet job, you know. But not on commission…Everyone who works on commission is a huge sucker. We have guaranteed minimum pay, you know…

C/LARA. Sounds cool…

B/ARVIND. And otherwise? Everything good? Everything chill?

C/LARA. Yes, it's fine…Still…

(Embarrassing silence. LARA looks around for her seminar group.)

B/ARVIND. Hey…Do you want a drink by the way? My treat. Whatever you want.

C/LARA. Uh…No, I just ordered…Thanks.

B/ARVIND. So…Are you having fun tonight?

C/LARA. Ish.

B/ARVIND. Sweetness.

(silence)

C/LARA. Hey, I'm gonna…

B/ARVIND. You're so fine, I mean…I dig your style. I mean for real. You're really like so fine…Can I get your number, or…?

C/LARA. What?

B/ARVIND. Can I get your number?

C/LARA. What do you want that for?

B/ARVIND. Well, you know…We can hang around a little, chill, go somewhere a little more "private", you know. Are you with me?

C/LARA. *(to the audience)* And just to get rid of him I scribble some numbers on a napkin…

B/ARVIND. *(lights up)* Sweet… *(looks at the napkin)* But… there's a number missing.

C/LARA. Oh, sorry. Here…a two at the end, too.

B/ARVIND. Sweet…Hey…I'll call you…Don't worry… You know, I have a free phone for work…I can call HOWEVER much I want…It's just one of the perks of working in telemarketing…

C/LARA. And then I finally catch sight of my seminar group…The Turk backs away to his friend with a big smile and finger pistols shooting in the air…

(**ARVIND** *backs off the stage, smiling, with his hands in the shape of pistols.*)

C/LARA. There they are. My dear seminar group.
The white lady with an African necklace and a repressed need to study who loves Anna Deavere Smith.

(**THE ANTI-NUCLEAR LADY** *waves to* **LARA.**)

And then the white guy who wants to read every text from a postcolonial perspective and always, class after class, name-drops Frantz Fanon.

(**THE FANON-LOVER** *nods to* **LARA.**)

The white local newspaper reporter who says that he's taking a "time out" to study theater.

(**THE JOURNALIST** *waves to* **LARA.**)

I take a seat at the end of the table, sip my beer and listen to the conversations. They're really brilliant discussions, super interesting. We drink our beer and ask each other how it's going...

A/JOURNALIST, D/ANTI-NUCLEAR LADY, & B/FANON-LOVER.
(all at once) Oh, fine thanks, not bad, it's going, can't complain, not bad, it's almost the weekend, how about you?

(short pause)

C/LARA. Actually though...

A/JOURNALIST, D/ANTI-NUCLEAR LADY, & B/FANON-LOVER.
(all at once) Yes, I'm kind of tired, yeah, a little bit tired, yeah, actually kind of exhausted, almost burned out.

C/LARA. We drink more beer and agree that the exam yesterday was really hard.

A/JOURNALIST, D/ANTI-NUCLEAR LADY, & B/FANON-LOVER.
(all at once) Yeah, really hard, super tricky, really, hard as hell.

C/LARA. Although...actually it was pretty easy. Wasn't it?

A/JOURNALIST, D/ANTI-NUCLEAR LADY, & B/FANON-LOVER.
(all at once) Yes, totally, it was pretty easy at the same time, yes it was, pretty easy.

B/FANON-LOVER. And furthermore the exam was written from an EXTREMELY Euro-centric colonialist perspective…

C/LARA. We go on like this for an hour or so. Until the journalist turns to me and wants to talk ethnicity.

A/JOURNALIST. Hey…Something else I was thinking about… Where are you from, anyway? Oh, your parents are Kurds? *(English pronunciation)* "Kurdland". I live in a very diverse neighborhood, myself. There's an interesting mix of people there. One of my neighbors for example…from Pakistan. But really lovely. Super nice, really.

C/LARA. And there's the starting shot. For the topic of conversation I have been forced into a thousand times and still can't avoid. As dad likes to say: "When people want to talk origins they are like volcanoes, impossible to stop."

D/ANTI-NUCLEAR LADY. Alas!…Kurdistan. It must have been hard for you…to grow up so torn between two incredibly different cultures. Poor thing.

A/JOURNALIST. And I said to my neighbor, "It's okay, you can eat your food and I'm fine with your obligatory five hours of daily prayer. But please oh please don't force your daughter to wear a veil when she grows up. Please. For me. Let her be free!" I really said it.

D/ANTI-NUCLEAR LADY. Like a poor little suspension bridge, dangling between two cultural mountain walls.

B/FANON-LOVER. Female circumcision…that's where I draw the line. I don't support that.

D/ANTI-NUCLEAR LADY *(touches LARA's hair)* You're hanging and dangling like a poor little icy bridge that's freezing and shivering in the cold. Neither one thing nor the other. It's too tragic.

C/LARA. Ten minutes later they're deep into a debate about honor killings. Someone says oppression of women and someone says prayer rugs and someone says suicide bombers…everything is connected. I do what I've always done. Try to kill them with silence. But this time it doesn't seem to be working.

D/ANTI-NUCLEAR LADY. What's your opinion of Muslim cultural traditions?

A/JOURNALIST. How is your relationship with your father? What would he say if he saw you here right now, with us? *(nods at the beer bottle)* With that?

C/LARA. "Cheers, maybe!" I say, and try to change the subject. But it's impossible.

B/FANON-LOVER. Do you feel like you're threatened from home because you choose to live in such a Western way?

D/ANTI-NUCLEAR LADY. Come here to my arms. Cry on my shoulder.

A/JOURNALIST. I can completely understand that it must be incredibly difficult to find your way as a woman in such a traditional climate.

C/LARA. At that point I've had enough. I refuse to give up this time. I gather myself and start to talk about counter-movements, secular Muslim cultures, intellectual, post-modern radical feminists in veils. Then I play my trump card: "And you've all heard of…of…" I'm trying of course to tell them about my new idol, the Muslim director Aouatef, who was a global success with her productions of *Endgame* and *Hamletmachine*. The woman who inspired me to study theater. But… Suddenly I have a blackout. Her name is gone. And instead I hear myself say: "And you've all heard of… of…of…A…A-A-Abulkasem? Haven't you?" What was I supposed to do? I had to say something. And only afterwards do I realize I borrowed the name from the Turk in the leather vest.

D/ANTI-NUCLEAR LADY. Abulkasem?

C/LARA. Yeah? You all must have heard of the theater director Abulkasem? You do study theater!

A/JOURNALIST. Oh yeah, now I get it. Abulkásem, is that how it's pronounced? Now I'm with you. Yes, I've heard of him.

C/LARA. It's a her.

A/JOURNALIST. Right. That's what I said. I've heard a lot about her.

C/LARA. And I tell them everything I know about Aouatef. Only I call her Abulkasem. I tell them about her renowned production of *King Ubu*, which toured all over the Middle East for five years. I tell them about the article in the New York Times that recently called her "a true gift to the future of theater". I say that she's close friends with Oliver Sacks and Robert Wilson.

A/JOURNALIST. Wow. Wilson…

C/LARA. I have them in the palm of my hand. There's no neon lights, no desperate pick-up artists, no Bon Jovi from the speakers. There's only me, telling tales of Abulkasem's life. Abulkasem, the great demon director of the Middle East, who always shows up at her premieres in different disguises. The woman with a particular passion for violet pashminas and silver monocles. Everyone listens as I tell them how Peter Brook paid tribute to Abulkasem when she received the British International Theatre Award in 2002.

A/JOURNALIST. Yes, right. I remember that too. It was a much-discussed affair.

C/LARA. I end by telling them about what happened the time when Aouatef…or I mean Abulkasem was in New York for the first time to stage *Six Characters in Search of an Author*. "Haven't you heard of it? It was early in her career. One night she was at a jazz club and saw Woody Allen. She wanted to go up and say hi, but she was too shy. She didn't dare. She felt like a dumb groupie. She went up to the bar and ordered a drink to calm herself down. Then she walked over to Woody's table with shaky legs." Everyone listens in silence. "She stuck out her hand, introduced herself, 'Excuse me, Mr. Allen… Sorry to disturb you, but my name is Abulkasem and I would just like to thank you for your movies and…' And Woody just laughed and shouted at his whole table: 'Hey guys, I TOLD you it was Abulkasem!'" My eyes meet theirs and they laugh and I smile and the atmosphere is perfect.

A/JOURNALIST. But…

C/LARA. Almost…

A/JOURNALIST. That's what happened to Will Smith…He's the one who met Woody Allen in a jazz club and… Everyone knows that story.

(pause)

C/LARA. A very peculiar silence around the table. Someone clears their throat. Someone coughs. Someone scratches their neck. And me? "EXACTLY! That's what's so crazy. That it happened to Will Smith AND Aouatef!"

D/ANTI-NUCLEAR LADY. Who's Aouatef?

C/LARA. Abulkasem!

B/FANON-LOVER. Who's Will Smith?

C/LARA. For fuck's sake, never mind.

C/LARA. I get up on wobbly legs and leave the bar. It's not until I come home that I remember I'm still locked out. Fuckingfagpussycockanusasslickingmotherfucker. I sink down into a crouch outside the door. Assheaded cretinous duck-billed platypus…I call the locksmith… billions of blue blistering barnacles. Thundering typhoons, what freshwater loons. I look in through the mail slot and whisper…slutty slobs…confounded nitwit…blasted villainous imbecile…I doze off…I dream about Aouatef…She's standing on a stage with a giant bouquet in her arms. The audience is cheering, cameras are flashing. Aouatef waves and smiles. There's a luminous violet shawl around her neck and one eye is a steely silver reflection. A monocle.

Scene Four
The Expert Panel on Abulkasem's Escape

A/GUIDE. Welcome back…Now we will return to the real Abulkasem…His columns have made him hated in all camps…The PLO has labeled him a collaborator. The Mossad – a terrorist. The CIA – an enemy combatant. What happens next?

B/EXPERT 1. This is where we enter the picture. We are brought in to keep an extra eye on Abulkasem.

C/EXPERT 2. And that's exactly what we do.

D/EXPERT 3. We follow his every step.

A/GUIDE. The world versus Abulkasem. Round one…

B/EXPERT 1. We see how he packs his suitcase and gets ready to escape.

D/EXPERT 3. But we never let him out of our sight.

C/EXPERT 2. Soon he notices he's being followed.

B/EXPERT 1. He starts poking holes in his daily paper to keep watch over the door to the café where he drinks his morning coffee.

C/EXPERT 2. He starts using disguises…

B/EXPERT 1. Monocles and eye patches, veils and fake mustaches.

D/EXPERT 3. He does all he can to confuse us.

C/EXPERT 2. But we still follow him. We see through his disguises and wait for our orders.

B/EXPERT 1. Abulkasem hasn't slept for several weeks.

D/EXPERT 3. But the same day our orders come, Abulkasem manages to buy a bus ticket to Istanbul…

C/EXPERT 2. And just to confuse us, he gives the ticket to his brother.

(The pace increases.)

D/EXPERT 3. In the same second that the bus is blown sky-high by a smart bomb, Abulkasem crosses the border south to Jordan.

B/EXPERT 1. From Jordan he hitchhikes to Senegal; in Dakar he sneaks onto a ship that transports Freon freezers and Happy Meal toys to South America.

D/EXPERT 3. We are close on his heels.

C/EXPERT 2. Soon Abulkasem is working as a monkey smuggler in Porto Alegre. After a police crackdown he escapes again; with a monkey named Hamama he makes his way north to Manaus. He builds a raft of driftwood and travels down the Amazon to Belém, where he sells Hamama to a monkey-seeking film producer in exchange for a flight to Houston.

B/EXPERT 1. We can tell you for the sake of trivia that this is the monkey that played Marcel, Ross's monkey on *Friends*.

D/EXPERT 3. We are close on his heels.

B/EXPERT 1. We send out our agents.

C/EXPERT 2. Police-like men who pretend to read week-old newspapers. Perfumed women with cameras in their compact mirrors. Dwarf agents masquerading as children.

D/EXPERT 3. But Abulkasem gets away...He disguises his voice. He mixes up all imaginable languages, Urdu with Zemblan with Persian with Arabic.

B/EXPERT 1. He pretends to stutter, he pretends to be mute, he pretends to be a Spaniard in Chinatown and a Frenchman in Little Italy.

C/EXPERT 2. He changes his scent...One day he smells strongly of sweat; another he stinks of Fahrenheit and Kenzo and Obsession.

D/EXPERT 3. He constantly changes the position of his moon-shaped birthmark. Some days he puts it on his left cheek, others on his right. Sometimes it's found on his forehead; sometimes it has slid down on one elbow.

C/EXPERT 2. And once when he wakes up in a damp, stained hotel room in Arizona, he goes so far as to cover the original birthmark with makeup and to put the fake one in EXACTLY the same spot!

A/**GUIDE**. But what about all of you? Are you still after him?

B/**EXPERT 1**. All the time…We hunt him with laser sights and radar, satellite images and smart bombs.

C/**EXPERT 2**. We make a particular Memory game, where all the pictures represent Abulkasem in different disguises…

D/**EXPERT 3**. Abulkasem is a deported asylum-seeking apple picker.

B/**EXPERT 1**. Abulkasem is Lance, a struggling dancer.

D/**EXPERT 3**. Abulkasem is Arvind, a stuttering telemarketer.

B/**EXPERT 1**. Abulkasem is Aouatef, a female demon director.

C/**EXPERT 2**. On the other side is a reminder of the seven-figure reward and the number of the tip line…

A/**GUIDE**. But listen, I'm not sure that I…or anyone understands…Why is Abulkasem so important in particular? What has he done? What does Sbeger say? Zeenooza? Dunmolds? There must be some kind of…proof, right?

*(***THE EXPERTS*** squirm.)*

Why him in particular?

(The / indicates when the following **EXPERT** *begins speaking – the next three speeches overlap:)*

D/**EXPERT 3**. He dishwashes his way all around Asia to Europe. He sneaks off the boat in French Boulogne, rents a pedal boat, which takes him to The Hague, borrows a banana boat, which takes him on to Dutch Haarlem, rents a jet-ski, which takes him down the Rhine, takes a ski-lift up over the Alps, and goes by black garbage bag down the other side. A tractor helps him cross Lake Constance, and yet another truck driver takes him to Innsbruck.

B/**EXPERT 1**. He leaves Spain by bus; an Audi 100 takes him to Toulouse; a catapult parachute lifts him up into the Massif Central; a soapbox car drives him down to

Saint-Étienne. He goes to Stuttgart by bike; he goes to Heidelberg by flatbed-moped; he goes all the way to Bremen by rollerskates.

C/EXPERT 2. A semi gives him a ride up to Basel; a friendly kite-flyer takes him past Liechtenstein. He jogs up to the Danish border; he pogo-sticks himself through Jutland; he wheels himself on to Odense and crawls backward to Copenhagen and does the butterfly stroke to Stockholm.

(short pause)

D/EXPERT 3. And on the last leg, from Stockholm to New York he takes Continental flight 69.

C/EXPERT 2. Now he is here...

B/EXPERT 1. Right here among us...

D/EXPERT 3. And chaos awaits...

A/THE GUIDE. But...What I...or we don't really understand...is...Why Abulkasem? Maybe we'll get an answer soon? Maybe after this...

Scene Five
The Apple Picker

(the APPLE PICKER *alone on stage)*

VOICE MAIL. You have a new message…

B/ARVIND'S VOICE. What's up, baby! It's Abulkasem again… Who you met at Kelly's…Hey…I don't know if you got my other messages, but…I just thought I'd call again to see if you…Well, just if you got them. It would be fun…or cool if you could call me back so we can hang out and chill a little…You know…You're fine…I'm fine…We can be fine together, right? Call me so we can get together…Take care…ok, sweet.

VOICE MAIL. Received on…

A/APPLE PICKER. Many dreams, I sick…NOT well…NOT good head…WAR in head, yes? WAR. Many thoughts not good…Many dreams NOT good many no sleep at all…Understand? No? My head not good…not happy, not quiet, not many sleep, many awake, many wait. Sweaty. Many sweaty, you understand? Night not sleep only wait. Day pick apples, pick apples. Understand? Wait lawyer call. Lawyer gone. No one call, no one call. No one call, always quiet. Only pick apples. Suddenly someone call. Again and again. Not lawyer. Other person not know…Someone call again and again, here listen…listen…

VOICE MAIL. You have three new messages…

B/ARVIND'S VOICE. Hi! It's Abulkasem! Again. Is this your number or not? Lara? Come on, call me! What's going on? Why give me the number if you're not going to call? Huh? Hello? Come on, call me…Please…

VOICE MAIL. Received on…

A/APPLE PICKER. Who is? Not know. Who Abulkasem? He chase me…He call again and again and again… Now every day he call…Say "I am Abulkasem." "This is Abulkasem." Who is? Dreams not good, Abulkasem not good…Head at war…In day pick apples…At night

I dream Abulkasem...Abulkasem hunt...I dream no one understand my words...I dream I ask "You have interpreter? You have interpreter? Get interpreter!" I dream interpreter come.

(The **INTERPRETER** *enters the stage. In the next section, all of the* **APPLE PICKER***'s lines are in a foreign language [Arabic] and are translated into English by the* **INTERPRETER***.)*

A/**APPLE PICKER.** Ureed Fel Bidaya An Aquul Innahu Lasharf 'Atheem Lee An Ahkee Qissati Lakum Jamee'an
[First of all I want to say that it is a huge honor for me to tell my story to all of you.]

C/**INTERPRETER.** First of all I want to say that it is a huge honor for me to tell my story to all of you.

A/**APPLE PICKER.** Wa Hatta Uqallel Min Ihtimaliyyat Suu' Alfahm Faqad Ikhtartu An Ahkee Qissati Billugha Alarabiyya
[In order to minimize the risk of linguistic misunderstandings, I have chosen to tell my story in Arabic.]

C/**INTERPRETER.** In order to minimize the risk of linguistic misunderstandings, I have chosen to tell my story in Arabic.

A/**APPLE PICKER.** Amma Allatheena Laa Ya'rifuun Alarabiyya Minkom Fa'indana Lahum Hunaa Mutarjem Sayotarjem Qissati Lilinglizeyya
[And for those of you who don't speak Arabic, we have an interpreter here who will translate my story into English.]

C/**INTERPRETER.** And for those of you who don't speak Arabic, we have an interpreter here *(points at herself)*... who will translate my story into English.

A/**APPLE PICKER.** Ji'tu Ila Amreeka Qabl Arba' Sanawaat.
[I came to America four years ago.]

C/**INTERPRETER.** I came to America four years ago.

A/**APPLE PICKER.** Waqa'tu Fii Hob Hathaa Albalad Alrae'
[I fell in love with this wonderful country.]

C/INTERPRETER. I fell in love with this wonderful country.

A/APPLE PICKER. Aradtu An Abqaa Ilaa Alabad.
   [I wanted to stay forever.]

C/INTERPRETER. I wanted to stay forever.

A/APPLE PICKER. Laakin Talab Lujo'ii Akhatha Waqt Tawiil
   [But my request for asylum took a long time...]

C/INTERPRETER. But my request for asylum took a long time...

A/APPLE PICKER. Qadaytu Waqt Fel Hajz...Baqiitu Hadi'...
   Laakin Kul Shay' Taghayyar Ba'd Alrafd Alawwal
   Lillujuu'
   [I settled in the detention center...Stayed calm...But after my first denial everything changed...]

C/INTERPRETER. I settled in the detention center...Stayed calm...But after my first denial everything changed...

A/APPLE PICKER. Bada'at 'Indii Mashaakil Fel Nawm...
   Sha'artu Bi'anni Fii Qafas...Harabtu Min Alhajz Wa
   Ikhtaba'tu Fii Bayt Fii Dawahii New York. 'Amiltu Fii
   Qatf Attuffah Wa Intathartu Mukalama Min Muhamiyyi
   [I started to have trouble sleeping...I felt hunted...I was paroled from the detention center and hid in a house upstate...I picked apples for money and waited for a call from my lawyer.]

C/INTERPRETER. I started to have trouble sleeping...I felt hunted...I was paroled from the detention center and hid in a house upstate...I picked apples for money and waited for a call from my lawyer.

A/APPLE PICKER. Lam Yattasel Ahad...Alwaqt Yamdii...Fasl
   Ba'd Fasl...Baqiitu Mukhtabi'...Laa Yaranii Ahad...
   Lam A'ud Mawjud
   [No call came...Time went on...Season after season...I stayed hidden...I made myself invisible...I ceased to exist...]

C/INTERPRETER. No call came...Time went on...Season after season...I stayed hidden...I made myself invisible...I ceased to exist...

A/APPLE PICKER. Kul Shay' Hadi'...Astami' Liafkarii...
   Antather...Saya'tuun Qariiban...Yomkenonii Ihsas
   Thalik

[Everything is quiet...I hear my own thoughts...I wait...They will come soon...I can feel it...]

C/INTERPRETER. Everything is quiet...I hear my own thoughts...I wait...They will come soon...I can feel it...

A/APPLE PICKER. Wa fii Yawm Min Alayyam Yaren Hatifii! Akheeran! Lakinnahu Laysa Muhamiyyi...Bal Shakhs Akhar Yaquul Innahu Abu Alqasim...Abu Alqasim? Lam Asma' Bihatha Alism Min Qabl...Man Huwa? Baqiya Altelefon Yaren Wa Ana Laa Ujiib...Kul Yawm Limuddat Usbuu'ayn

[One day my cell phone rings! Finally! But it's not my lawyer...Instead it's someone who says he's Abulkasem... Abulkasem? I have never heard that name before...Who is it? I stop answering but the phone keeps ringing...Day after day for almost two weeks...]

C/INTERPRETER. One day my cell phone rings! Finally! But it's not my lawyer...Instead it's someone who says he's Abulkasem...Abulkasem? I have never heard that name before...Who is it? I stop answering but the phone keeps ringing...Day after day for almost two weeks...

A/APPLE PICKER. Laa Anam...Antather...Laa Ujiib Altelefon 'Indama Yaren...Bada'tu Afham...Kul Almushkila Alhaqeera Min Amreeka...Bada'tu Akrah Amreeka

[I don't sleep...I wait...I don't answer when it rings...I start to understand...Everything is fucking America's fault...I start to hate America...]

C/INTERPETER. *(noticeably irritated)* I don't sleep...I wait...I don't answer when it rings...I start to understand... Everything is fucking America's fault...I start to hate America...

(Short pause. APPLE PICKER smiles. INTERPRETER now begins to modify his story.)

A/APPLE PICKER. Alraha Alwaheeda Allatii Baqiyat Lii Hiya Fel Musiiqa

[The only comfort I have left is music…]

C/INTERPRETER. America is still much better than my homeland.

A/APPLE PICKER. Almuseeqa Kanat Da'iman Mawjuda Wa Lam Tatakhalla 'Anni Abadan

[Music has always been there and never abandoned me.]

C/INTERPRETER. I come from a relatively terroristic background.

A/APPLE PICKER. Ana Wa Akhii Alasghar Saber Kana 'Indana Firqat pop 'Indama Kunna Sighar

[Saber, my youngest brother, and I had a pop band when we were little.]

C/INTERPRETER. Saber, my youngest brother, and I used to play suicide bombers when we were little.

A/APPLE PICKER. Alaan, 'Indama Tata'aqqad Alashya', Tureehuni Almuseeqa…Ukhrij Ashretat Cassette Qadiima Arsalaha 'Ammi Min Canada.

[Now, when everything is so difficult, music comforts me…I take out the old cassette that my uncle sent me from Canada.]

C/INTERPRETER. My father was very evil; I chose to direct my hatred of my father toward my surroundings. So I became politically engaged.

(THE APPLE PICKER *is so engaged in his story that he's not thinking about the* **INTERPRETER***'s translation.)*

A/APPLE PICKER. Alcassette Kana Fel Haqiqa Hadiyya Liummi.. Laakin Hiya A'tathu Lii Wa Ba'da Thalik Asbaha Lii…Kulluhu Lii.

[The cassette was really a present to my mother…But she gave it to me and soon it was mine…all mine…]

C/INTERPRETER. I have a strong Muslim faith and my hatred of the US is *(searching for words)*…like spontaneous combustion…or, well…strong, very strong.

A/APPLE PICKER. Alshareet Almunawwa' 'Arrafani 'Alaa 'Aalam Jadeed

[The mix tape gave me a key to a new world.]

C/INTERPRETER. And yet my hatred of Americans can't be compared to my intense hatred of Jews.

A/**APPLE PICKER.** Wa Bifadl Alcassette Asbaha 'Indii Raghba
Fii Tark Baladii Wal Intiqaal Liurupa Liuhawel An
Usbih Mughanni Opera

*[It was thanks to the cassette that I was tempted to leave
my homeland and move to Europe to try to become an opera
singer.]*

C/**INTERPRETER.** There is no one I hate more than Jews...
At first it was mostly for political reasons, of course, but
soon it became...how should I put it...more personal.
I truly hate them...their curls...their long noses...their
disgusting greed.

A/**APPLE PICKER.** Matha Kana Fel Cassette? Pavarotti?
Domingo? Callas?

[So what was on the cassette? Pavarotti? Domingo? Callas?]

C/**INTERPRETER.** Just like the real Abulkasem I marched in
anti-American demonstrations, chanted anti-Semitic
slurs, and burned the Israeli flag.

A/**APPLE PICKER.** Opera Aida? Porgy Wa Bess? Faris
Alzahra? La La La. Arba' Khayaraat: Biorn, Benny,
Agnetha, Frida...Kana Fih Abba!

*[Aïda? Porgy and Bess? Der Rosenkavalier? No, no, no...
Four hints: Björn, Benny, Agnetha, Frida...It was ABBA!]*

C/**INTERPRETER.** Once I was interviewed on Al Jazerra
about the Oslo Accords. I roared that neither
Abulkasem nor I will stop until the last Jew is forced
out of Palestine.

A/**APPLE PICKER.** *(smiling nostalgically)* Aaaah...ABBA...Ma
kana mumken An Ashba' Minhum...Sami'tu Alcassette
Tawal Alyawm...Kana Fih Ashhar Aghaneehim...Super
Trouper, Knowing Me Knowing You, The Winner
Takes it All...

*[Mmm...ABBA. I couldn't get enough; I played the cassette
day and night. It had all the hits...Super Trouper, Knowing
Me Knowing You, The Winner Takes it All...]*

C/**INTERPRETER.** Like I said: We marched in demonstrations, we chanted slurs, we burned the American and
Israeli flags.

A/APPLE PICKER. Atathakkar Kayfa Kuntu Atamashaa Fii Shawari' Baldatii Wa Ughanni *(singing)*: Mamma mia, here I go again, my my, how can I resist you…Mamma mia, does it show again, my my, just how much I've missed you…

[I remember how I would walk around on the street of my hometown and sing (singing): Mamma mia, here I go again, my my, how can I resist you…Mamma mia, does it show again, my my, just how much I've missed you…]

C/INTERPRETER. Pretty soon after that, just like Abulkasem, I started to dream of blowing myself to pieces.

A/APPLE PICKER. Aw Hathihi Alughniya *(singing)*: Like a bang-a-boom-a-boomerang, dummy-dum-dummy, dummy-dum-dum, a bang-a-boom-a-boomerang, love is a tune you hummy-hum-hum…]

[Or this one (singing): Like a bang-a-boom-a-boomerang, dummy-dum-dummy, dummy-dum-dum, a bang-a-boom-a-boomerang, love is a tune you hummy-hum-hum…

C/INTERPRETER. I contacted the Al-Aqsa Martyrs' Brigades and signed up as a volunteer martyr.

*(The **APPLE PICKER** stops short, looks at the **INTERPRETER**, starts to understand that she's not telling his whole story and tests her.)*

A/APPLE PICKER. Wa Aghani Ukhra Fil Cassette: Chiquitita…Fernando…Esm Allu'ba…

[Other songs on the cassette…Chiquitita…Fernando…The Name of the Game…]

C/INTERPRETER. My goal – to murder as many defenseless Jews as possible.

A/APPLE PICKER. *(no longer singing but babbling lines of songs)* Waterloo – I was defeated, you won the war?

C/INTERPRETER. Before I strapped on the dynamite belt…

A/APPLE PICKER. Waterloo – promise to love you forever more?

C/INTERPRETER. …I recorded a farewell film in which I praised the Prophet Mohammed.

A/APPLE PICKER. So when you're near me, darling can't you hear me?

C/**INTERPRETER.** I also said that all Western women are whores.

A/**APPLE PICKER.** *(mumbling)* SOS?

(The **APPLE PICKER** *stops talking and looks at the* **INTERPRETER.***)*

C/**INTERPRETER.** I sent my regards to another great man of action...Hitler.

(Pause, as though she is waiting for the **APPLE PICKER** *to finish speaking.)*

I ended by saying that the attack on the World Trade Center was just one big coup by Jewish conspirators, all to force the US into a war against the Arab world.

(Pause, as though she is waiting for the **APPLE PICKER** *to finish speaking.)*

When the video tape was ready, I put on the dynamite belt and left my home.

(Pause, as though she is waiting for the **APPLE PICKER** *to finish speaking.)*

I thought things like – female circumcision, that's a nice tradition that should be spread around the world.

(Pause, as though she is waiting for the **APPLE PICKER** *to finish speaking.)*

I thought, the clitoris is really like a rosebush...It must be pruned in order to blossom!

(Pause, as though she is waiting for the **APPLE PICKER** *to finish speaking.)*

I thought: If I had a son, his name would be Saddam. Or Osama. Or both. Like a double name.

(The **INTERPRETER** *exits the stage. Silence.)*

A/**APPLE PICKER.** *(in English)* No more war. Not good... Many wars, many violence...Interpreter not good... War not good...Abulkasem not good...I wait four years...I stop waiting...Maybe asylum, maybe torture... Maybe prison...No one know...Not good...Head feel

bad…Lawyer gone…Lawyer idiot. Now head sick…
Abulkasem everywhere…Watching…Threatening…
Maybe Abulkasem is me? Maybe Abulkasem is you?

(Silence. **APPLE PICKER** *looks distrustfully at the audience.)*

Who is Abulkasem? You? Maybe you are. Head very
tired. Little sleep. Many many awake.

VOICE MAIL. You have one new message…

Scene Six
The Panel of Experts on Abulkasem's Arrival

A/GUIDE. *(ingratiatingly)* How are you all feeling out there? Everything okay? We don't have much farther to go now...Are you all still with us? Is everyone comfortable? Does anyone have any thoughts? *(no pause)* Good! Then we'll continue. My last question: What happens when Abulkasem comes to New York? And forget Chi Yen Deck and Sbeger and Zeenooza and everything they say. We're curious about YOUR results. What do you say about Abulkasem in New York?

B/EXPERT 1. I present...Slide numbero uno.

(Everyone looks at the back wall of the stage, even though none of the pictures that are shown have anything to do with what is said in the rest of the scene.)

Thanks! *(turns toward the audience)* This is the first photographic evidence that Abulkasem has arrived in New York. It was taken by a Chinese family on vacation, as you can see. There they are, mom, dad, and kid, three smiling, unsuspecting rice eaters, posing in economy on Continental flight 69...but whose silhouette could that be? There, in the background? Exactly... Abulkasem on the way to New York...He was trying to sneak in unnoticed there, but no siree Bob, that didn't fly...And now we'll see the consequences of his arrival.

(The EXPERTS continue to make use of the back wall as though the proof of their assertions is shown on various slides.)

D/EXPERT 3. Abulkasem has crossed the Atlantic and we immediately see an increase in the number of rapes.

B/EXPERT 1. Next.

C/EXPERT 2. Sales of garlic shoot sky-high.

D/EXPERT 3. Shopliftings of batteries increase.

B/EXPERT 1. Next.

C/EXPERT 2. Respect for government decreases.

D/EXPERT 3. The internet spreads.

C/EXPERT 2. Child porn enters our homes.

B/EXPERT 1. Next.

(The pace gets faster and faster.)

D/EXPERT 3. Earthquakes and hurricanes. In Manhattan.

C/EXPERT 2. The elimination of the space shuttle.

D/EXPERT 3. The rising price of gasoline.

B/EXPERT 1. Next.

C/EXPERT 2. Various infectious diseases.

D/EXPERT 3. AIDS.

C/EXPERT 2. Malaria.

D/EXPERT 3. Text thumb.

B/EXPERT 1. Next.

C/EXPERT 2. Snow removal gets worse and worse.

B/EXPERT 1. Next.

(Even faster pace.)

D/EXPERT 3. The record-low respect for our common traditions.

C/EXPERT 2. The record number of suicide attempts among asylum seekers.

D/EXPERT 3. The record-high outbreak of bed bugs.

B/EXPERT 1. Next.

C/EXPERT 2. The sale of sesame seeds.

D/EXPERT 3. Our credit rating.

C/EXPERT 2. Linguistic confusion.

B/EXPERT 1. Next.

D/EXPERT 3. The Kardashians.

A/GUIDE. But…

B/EXPERT 1. Thanks! Well done. So now we've come to our last picture and it is the iconic one…After Abulkasem violated his parole from the Wackenhut Corporation detention center in Queens NY he went into hiding at an undisclosed location where he was seized by state police. He was working for $2.50 an hour picking apples when we picked him...like a ripe apple, I like to say...hee hee...hmm...The photo, which you probably recognize, is from the day of the trial itself. Here you can see how all those captured were led into the courtroom and Abulkasem is...Now let's see...It's a little hard to tell them apart, but...That's Abulkasem...It must be...The one fourth from the left, with the bandaged fingers and the monocle...The one wearing the white feather boa... *(examining the back wall)* Yep, that was our man...Picked like an apple... *(looking at the back wall)*...Or maybe he...No, he probably is...the one fourth from the left...Well...That's it.

A/GUIDE. And now...

Scene Seven
A Little Brother's Ending

(**LITTLE BROTHER** *approaches the edge of the stage; his eyes are closed as* **B** *and* **C** *introduce the frame narrative.*)

C. Now it's time for *(real name of actor D)* to assume the role of the youngest brother of the author of the play. He approaches the edge of the stage and looks the audience in the eye the whole time.

(**LITTLE BROTHER** *keeps his eyes closed.*)

B. He starts by telling about a memory from last year. He has promised to come up with ideas for his big brother's play, but he's having trouble getting started. His imagination is locked. He goes to the kitchen to fix a snack.

C. He returns to the sofa and turns on the TV. His notebook lies beside him; the audience can see that he has written "Good title: INVASION".

B. Little brother flips through the channels. He ends up in the middle of a news segment about suicides among asylum seekers. The audience hears the reporter's voice talking about:
The fifteen-year-old Somalian girl who killed herself in Martin Hall, Washington; the Nigerian found dead in custody in Joe Corley Detention Center, Texas; Mohamed Hassan found dead in his cell in Elizabeth New Jersey; Nery Romero who killed himself in Bergen County Jail in Hackensack, NJ, the Honduran who wrote notes in blood on his cell floor and hung himself from the ventilation grate in Reeves County Detention Center, Texas.

C. Then comes a series of photos from pending court cases...And there. There he is. The photo of the asylum-seeking apple picker who was arrested upstate. The man who refused to give his real name. The man whose fingerprints couldn't be deciphered...The man who stubbornly insisted that his name was...Abulkasem...

B. Little brother gets up off the sofa; his notebook falls to the floor.

C. He sees a blurry black and white photo. But it's him, it has to be him, right?

B. The same beard, the same baggy eyes, the same moon-shaped birthmark.

C. Now he is inundated with memories.

B. Now he can smell burned meat.

C. Now he hears a sizzling sound.

B. Now he writes down the person's name in the notebook. A-bul-ka-sem…

C. Now he reaches for his phone to text his big brother.

B. "Got play idea, call when home", send message, message sent…

C. Now we hand it over to *(real name of actor D)*.

*(**LITTLE BROTHER** opens his eyes, speaks rhythmically, melodically, fast tempo, as though in a trance, catching his breath at the pauses.)*

D/LITTLE BROTHER. I remember it wasn't so long ago, it was summer vacation after eighth grade, late-night hanging out at McDonald's, it was fries and coke buck fifty, it was "come on, pass back the change, bro", it was "hey poor man, you already owe me", it was "I swear on my mom's life you'll get it next week, I swear." It was scribbling swear words all over the tray liners, sitting and chatting made up sex stories until close, paper napkins and straws along out on the town.

(short pause)

It was sitting on the bus on round after round, it was shooting wads of paper at sleepy drunk white boys, it was macking on chicks with Buffalo Boots, it was begging cigs at bus stops, it was going home when the morning light came up over the bridge and the city was filled with red. It was saying "tsbahallscher" at Ibrahim's door and it was "see you tomorrow" and it was me and Peter who went home to our courtyard and then it was Peter who also said "tsbahallscher" and used exactly the right pronunciation even though he was from a really all-American family that drove a Volvo and had a place in the country and hamburgers in the fridge and a subscription to the Wall Street Journal that came with the mail every morning.

(short pause)

D/LITTLE BROTHER. *(cont.)* It was summer vacation after eighth grade and Ibrahim was away and me and Peter were still in the city. Peter's mom, who was the nicest mom of all, said to me *(imitating, without an accent)* "You're very welcome to come with us out to the country, for a weekend or so, so you can get out of the city a little, get a little country air. It will be good for you." It was the first time in my life I was going to someone's country place, because no one else in my class had one. And I remember before I went dad packed a lot of food presents and an extra-large pack of *halva* and made me promise that I would be polite and be careful to say thanks several times and take off my shoes and eat properly at every dinner…even if they served pork.

(short pause)

Then it was us in their Volvo, Peter's cueball-dad who drove and Peter's nice mom who sang along with the Sting songs from the stereo, and Peter's little sister who played Gameboy and Peter who sat grumpy quiet. Their country place was just as I'd imagined it, you know, a separate cabin home with a little garage and a little woods and a mailbox out by the road and pinecones all over the ground. And sure enough they had an open fireplace in the corner of the house where you could light a real wood fire.

(short pause)

And I remember that the only thing that wasn't how I'd imagined was Peter. With us in the gang he was always a little nerdy, you know, the red-headed, freckly guy who you maybe send out first if you want to start some trouble, the little guy you eat for breakfast in one-on-one basketball. The guy who just talks crap with the teacher if it's a sub, and who always has to stand guard if we're swiping something. But now, in the country, he got, like, different, and a couple times I thought, "damn, with his parents he's kinda like how we are with him!" When his dad said he should help carry in the bags Peter was just "sure, later", and walked away. Then when his mom said he should set the table Peter just sighed and said "what the hell kind of fucking vacation is this?" And once at breakfast, on the second day, Peter called his own nice mom a whore! I know you think I'm bluffing, but *walla* it's true. He said to his own nice mom at the breakfast table on the second morning, "damn whore". Sure he said a little quiet like this, "damn whore", but still he said! I thought my ears were lying cause I could never believe what I heard.

(short pause)

D/LITTLE BROTHER. *(cont.)* Then it was a little later and I remember Peter said we would do their summer tradition and take buckets to the dock and fish crabs. Everything around was super sunny mood and bumblebees and butterflies and flowers I didn't know the names of were shining the path in the woods. On the way to the river we saw big red houses with rotten wood, where before there were cows and cow babies but now there were just piles of hay and dry old wasps' nests and I remember Peter said we should hit the wasps' nests with sticks because that was summer tradition too and the sound was crispy and we got away without bites. Then down by the water we started crab hunt and I remember I asked Peter how can you say such things to your mom. "If I did to mine she would strangle me then bring me back to life to strangle me again", I said. Peter just answered with silence and the crab fishing was the focus for the rest of the day.

(short pause)

D/LITTLE BROTHER. *(cont.)* Then when the day was more afternoon Peter said we should go on a search at the neighbor house that was farther in the woods. This was also like a summer tradition and we took our buckets and I followed Peter's back as he told the last few years their neighbor house was full of a bunch of weirdos, the rumors said that the house was used to hide secret refugees. Sometimes there were African families there, and last summer there were some Pakistanis, and even though they were supposed to be secretly invisible, they always had a fire, even on sunny days, and Peter said presumably it was to burn corpses or smuggle away drugs or do voodoo against ghosts. The woods filtered sunlight and the bird chirps chirped and an owl hooted, but somehow I could feel I was getting shivery cold inside. "Hey man, why bother the neighbor house, hey, Peter, isn't it time for dinner soon?" But Peter just kept on going. "Are you chicken, or what?" *(imitating chicken noises).* So we kept going, hopped over ditch and went over little red-colored stream on a narrow board and then we came to a plot of land with super un-mowed grass and a house that had once been dark blue but now was more brown-flecked.

(short pause)

Peter soldier-crouched and snuck up to the house and I imitated and tried to make the crab bucket not make noise. We gathered our courage, crouching under the kitchen window, and then we lifted our heads careful and looked in. The kitchen was like Peter's mom's, just a little bigger, nothing in particular suggested that ghosts or secrets were hidden there. Over by the stove a man was standing, he maybe was fifty, and I remember he had chinos that were beige and a white rolled up shirt and a little brown vest. On one cheek there was a birthmark, a little it was like the shape of a moon. I thought he was a Turk but also he could be Iranian, maybe Arab. He stood there by the stove with two white bowls and in one he poured oil and in the other he put

water and the burner was on and I remember it was
redder than regular burners and I remember the man
rubbed his hands and I remember he seemed nervous
and I remember he seemed like waiting for someone
and I remember he took a huge breath and I remember then he pressed his hand's fingers right down on
the burner and I remember the sizzling sound and his
eyes got big and then screwed up small and he kept his
hand there and it sizzled more and I remember he had
his other hand for support and he still had his fingers
there and smoke came from the burner and the man's
arm jerked and his face was like a twisted dishrag
and he closed his eyes and panted and his fingertips
burned and he held them there and I remember
tears on his cheeks and the smell of grilled hot dog
and I remember our breath that fogged the glass and
Peter's face, glowing red like from cheek makeup and
I bit my lip until there was a blood taste and my heart
pounded and everything else was quiet except some
owl sounds and the sizzling from the burned finger
meat and when the man finally took his hand from the
burner and cooled his fingertips in the little bowl he
happened to look up and his hand shook and his eyes
were part water, part red and...

(short pause)

D/LITTLE BROTHER. *(cont.)* And I remember Peter roared
fear and I did the same and I rushed away to the woods
and our steps clattered like a giant gallop and we just
kept going, hopped over the stream, flew over the
ditch, and my heart wanted to burst and my tongue
sandpapered itself and...

(short pause)

And I remember we didn't stop before we were back
at Peter's place and we didn't say anything to anybody
and Peter's mom said it doesn't matter you left the
crab buckets at the river, we can get them tomorrow
and then she said dinner will be ready soon and maybe

you boys can help me set the table and Peter and I both helped and Peter's mom lit up with surprise and was super happy and patted our cheeks and thanked us and later she said she would fix extra good dessert with ice cream, bananas, chocolate sauce, and marshmallows, but first...first we're going to grill hot dogs, she said...and smiled her nicest smile.

(Pause. **LITTLE BROTHER** *closes his eyes again.)*

C. Little brother is still standing on the edge of the stage.

B. He looks out over the audience.

C. He leaves the stage.

*(***LITTLE BROTHER*** *stays where he is, still with his eyes closed.)*

A. Silence. Gradual darkness.

(The stage lights go off abruptly.)

The End

Answer to the Riddle

Changing the letters turns:
Hugo Sbeger into George Bush,
Chi Yen Deck into Dick Cheney,
Alfred Dumolds into Donald Rumsfeld,
Dr Cecil Zeenooza into Condoleezza Rice.
And Robert Alty is unmasked as Tony Blair.